HEROES OF GOTHAM CITY

adapted by J. E. Bright   illustrated by Patrick Spaziante
Based on the screenplay *Animal Instincts* written by Heath Corson
Batman created by Bob Kane with Bill Finger

Ready-to-Read

Simon Spotlight
New York   London   Toronto   Sydney   New Delhi

SIMON SPOTLIGHT
An imprint of Simon & Schuster Children's Publishing Division
1230 Avenue of the Americas, New York, New York 10020
This Simon Spotlight edition August 2016. All rights reserved, including the right of
reproduction in whole or in part in any form. SIMON SPOTLIGHT, READY-TO-READ,
and colophon are registered trademarks of Simon & Schuster, Inc.
For information about special discounts for bulk purchases, please
contact Simon & Schuster Special Sales at 1-866-506-1949 or
business@simonandschuster.com.
Manufactured in the United States of America 1216 LAK
10 9 8 7 6 5 4 3 2
ISBN 978-1-4814-7722-2 (hc)
ISBN 978-1-4814-7721-5 (pbk)
ISBN 978-1-4814-7723-9 (eBook)

Mayday! Mayday!
Gotham City is under attack!
It's up to Batman
and his super hero team
to save the day.

Meet Nightwing.
Nightwing is a skilled fighter.
He was trained by Batman.

Nightwing arrives
outside of a jewelry store.
Bam! Someone is breaking in.
It's the villain Cheetah!
Nightwing follows her inside.

"Hold it right there,"
Nightwing says.
He stops Cheetah from stealing
some priceless jewels.

But Cheetah is fast.
She pins Nightwing to the ground.
"I think not," she says.

Nightwing is quick too.
He grabs his electric clubs and
zaps Cheetah!
"Shocking, right?" Nightwing says.
Cheetah is knocked out!

Meanwhile, The Flash bursts in.
He has come at a very good time.
The villain Killer Croc
has also arrived.

The Flash jabs at him so quickly,
Killer Croc has no idea
what's going on.
"I'm the Fastest Man Alive,"
says The Flash.
He can race up buildings,
dash across water,
and even run around the world!

The Flash is funny, too.
"Man, you smell,"
he tells Killer Croc.
"When is the last time you bathed?"
He takes Killer Croc down.

The Flash used to be a scientist,
but then he was struck by lightning.
The lightning gave him super-speed.
Now The Flash uses his superpower
to protect people.

Green Arrow is secretly
Oliver Queen, a billionaire.
When Oliver was stranded on a
deserted island, he learned
skills like archery.
Green Arrow protects people too.
He likes to say,
"Impossible is my middle name!"

Green Arrow shoots different kinds
of arrows with special tips.
Some of his arrows have
boxing gloves,
some have smoke, and some
cause so much noise
they knock their opponents out.

Green Arrow takes on a villain
that looks like a giant ape.
"I am Silverback. You are toast!"
the ape yells.
He fires his lasers at Green Arrow.

But Silverback is no match
for Green Arrow. *Boing!*
Green Arrow uses his expert
archery skills to fire an arrow
into Silverback's laser.
It's destroyed.
"Bull's-eye," Green Arrow says.

Red Robin is being trained by
none other than Batman.
He kicks at two robots
in the training arena.
"Did you see that combo?"
Red Robin asks.

"Yeah, you're still dropping
your shoulder," Batman says.
It is hard work to train
to be a super hero.

Batman would know.
Secretly, he is Bruce Wayne,
a billionaire and CEO
of Wayne Enterprises.
Batman defends Gotham City
with his strength, his wit,
and his high-tech gadgets.

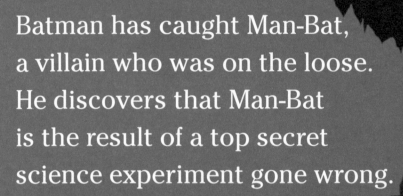

Batman has caught Man-Bat,
a villain who was on the loose.
He discovers that Man-Bat
is the result of a top secret
science experiment gone wrong.

Beneath Man-Bat's scary
appearance is a scientist by the
name of Dr. Kirk Langstrom.

Batman creates an antidote to turn
Man-Bat back into Dr. Langstrom,
but it lasts only for three hours.

Grateful to be human again,
Dr. Langstrom explains that
when he is Man-Bat,
he is controlled by a villain
named the Penguin.
The Penguin is behind the attacks
by Cheetah, Killer Croc,
and Silverback, too.

The super heroes head out
to stop the Penguin
from attacking the city again.
But since the antidote has worn off,
Red Robin stays behind
to guard Man-Bat.

Scree!
Oh no.
The chamber isn't strong enough
to hold Man-Bat.
He breaks out.
He wants to find
and help the Penguin.

Red Robin isn't fast like The Flash,
or an expert archer
like Green Arrow,
or an athlete like Nightwing,
but Red Robin is brave.

"Dr. Langstrom,
I can't let you do this,"
Red Robin says.
He flips onto Man-Bat's back
and gets dragged away.

Man-Bat carries Red Robin
high above the city.
"Dr. Langstrom," Red Robin says.
"Your body has changed,
but not your mind!"

Then something amazing happens.
Man-Bat's eyes go wide.
He may be Man-Bat on the outside,
but he's still Dr. Langstrom
on the inside!
Man-Bat will help the super heroes
stop the Penguin.

With Man-Bat on their side,
the super heroes use their
special skills to put an end
to the Penguin's evil plan.
Good-bye to the Penguin!

Man-Bat even transforms back
into Dr. Langstrom!
"Thank you, Batman,"
Dr. Langstrom says.
"Thank you for
giving me my life back."
Once again, the super heroes
of Gotham City have saved the day!